TALES OF

The Legend of Gobán

GERARD RONAN

Illustrated by Derry Dillon

libraries.
fingal.ie

ISBN: 9781914348013

CONTENTS

THE BIRTH OF GOBÁN

A LONG, LONG time ago, about one hundred years after the time of Saint Patrick, there lived a tall, dark-haired warrior with exceptionally large feet. His name was Tuirbe Tragmár, and he lived behind the grassy mounds of his family's fort on a windswept peninsula that reached out into the Irish Sea west of Lambay Island.

Tuirbe lived according to the old ways and worshipped the old gods. It was how his father and grandfather had lived, and how he intended to bring up his children. In times of peace he made his living as a farmer and a hunter, but in times of war, or when other clans attempted to steal his cattle, he became a warrior so fearsome in battle that people believed him to be protected by the battle goddess, Morrigan.

Loved by his friends, and feared by his enemies, Tuirbe had come to be known as the guardian of his clan. And yet, for all his hair-raising exploits, he would always be remembered more for his famous axe than for his courage. Even the hill upon which he would later be buried would be called 'The Hill of the Axe' rather than 'Tuirbe's Hill'.

Tuirbe was tall and strong. Indeed it was said that he was so strong that he once threw his axe into the sea from the top of this very same hill. If you live near to the village of Portrane, you might know this place. It is where St. Ita's Hospital stands today and it sits roughly the length of seven football pitches from the sea. That is a very long way for a person to throw an axe, and it is why the hill was for so long known as *Tuladh an*

Bhiail or the 'Hill of the Axe'.

Tuirbe's axe was a weapon unlike any that had ever been seen before, or would ever be seen again. It had been forged in the far distant past by Gobniu, the god of metalworking. To spite Lir, the god of the sea, Gobniu had given this axe the power to stop the incoming tide. To a man who lived on a coastal peninsula, and whose lands were often flooded by high tides, this was a very useful and valuable property indeed.

Now it happened one day, while Tuirbe was still a young man, that his wife, Dearbhail, gave birth to a son. Born with a head of hair as red as molten metal, he was given the name Gobán and he grew up to be very special. Like all young boys of that time, he spent the days of his childhood learning to throw spears, to lay traps and snares, and to fish. At times, he would also assist his sisters in the collecting of mussels and the making of hazelnut mead.

In most respects, Gobán was a boy like any

other, forever wrestling with his friends, pulling girls' hair, and never managing to keep his clothes clean. As for the places he would put his finger and the things he would put in his mouth, it is perhaps better not to mention such things, as you may be eating while you are reading this.

At the age of twelve, as was customary amongst his people, Gobán was allowed to enter the ranks of the hunters. This was the standard coming-of-age ritual of the time and it meant that Gobán was recognised by his clan as being no longer a child, but a youth on the threshold of manhood.

Before he could undergo his coming-of-age ceremony, however, Gobán had to learn how to navigate by the stars, how to train and handle his wolfhounds, and how to recognise the sounds of all the birds and animals. Only then, when he had proven his knowledge of nature, would his skill with a bow and spear be tested by his elders.

Having passed all of the tests that had been

set for him, Gobán was invited to a ceremony where he was anointed with oil, presented with a set of newly forged weapons, and invited to recite the most sacred oath of the hunter.

'I swear by Cernunnos the Horned,' declared Gobán, 'God of wild things and Lord of man and nature, that I shall never take a life without good reason, nor kill a sitting bird, nor a beast lying down, nor the mother of a brood or sucklings, nor an unfledged bird, nor any suckling beast unless it be a bird or beast of prey. These things I, Gobán son of Tuirbe, do swear for life.'

The path of his future life, it seemed, had been set. He would follow in his father's footsteps, his parents would choose a wife for him, and he would inherit his father's lands when he died.

But Gobán never became a hunter, for it was not to be his calling. As the notches that marked his annual gain in height began to race up the doorpost, he began, somewhat surprisingly, to show a flair for metalworking and carpentry. A clever and curious pupil, he was quick to master every skill he turned his hand to, a fact that surprised nobody, for it was well known that he had come from a long line of artists and learned men.

Many generations before Gobán's birth, a man by the name of Lugh had arrived one day at the court of the High King of Ireland at Tara. Lugh was what they called a *Samildánach* – a man skilled in *all* of the arts and sciences. Indeed, so quickly did he secure the High King's favour, that the king came to rely more on *his* judgement than the judgement of the many artists and learned men of his own court.

Slighted by the King's neglect, this group of the cleverest and most talented men in Ireland decided to abandon the royal court and to take themselves off to the hazel woods of Fingal, where they settled. As Gobán's mother was a descendant of one of this ancient band, it came as no surprise to his people to find that, as he grew into his adult body, the gods should have other plans for Gobán.

Gobán, you see, had been blessed with a gift even more powerful than his father's famous axe – a fertile imagination. How he loved to build things! As a child, he would sit for hours watching local craftsmen as they worked, never disturbing them with questions or taking his eyes off their hands. Through observation alone, he mastered their crafts and by the time he was fifteen had surpassed them all.

Nobody worked better or faster than Gobán. He could fashion a spear shaft in the time it took to boil an egg and shape an axe head with just seven blows of a hammer. And yet, for all his great talents, there was not a single craftsman that ever resented Gobán's gift, for the boy was also kind and modest, a source of pride to his clan and a reminder of their glorious past.

It did not take Tuirbe long to recognise his son's genius, for where others made things as they had always been made, Gobán would invent new methods and produce work of extraordinary quality. Some people even began to believe that he had been given the gift of foresight.

His thirst for learning never satisfied, Gobán was forever experimenting with twigs and stones, making small models of houses, bridges and furniture. He loved the thrill of discovery when one of his experimental models actually worked. It was, perhaps, his greatest joy.

Now it happened one summer, while he was still a teenager and anxious to impress his father, that Gobán came to build a giant wooden chest. It sat on four legs like a cabinet and was a masterpiece of carpentry many centuries ahead of its time. Not a single nail had been used in the making of it, and so smoothly had the joints been shaped and planed that it appeared to have been carved from a single piece of wood.

'What do you think, Father?' asked Gobán when

the chest was completed. 'Do you like it?'

'It's as fine a piece of carpentry as I have ever seen,' said Tuirbe, glowing with pride, 'and I am certain that someone will have a use for it. Take it to the market at Swords. Perhaps someone will trade with you, or ask you to make another.'

'Really?' said Gobán. 'The market?'

'Why not?' said Tuirbe. 'You must surely get a cow for such a fine chest and, seeing as our annual tribute of cattle is due to be paid shortly to the king, a cow would be a fair and timely price to ask.'

That afternoon Gobán strapped the chest to the back of an old black ox and took it to the market at the village of Swords. But the reception he got was far from the one he had been expecting, for perfection often offends the eye and people love to find fault.

The first man who stopped to examine the wooden chest declared, 'It's a fine chest to be sure, Gobán, and no one could have made it but yourself. But it's a bit too low.'

His confidence shaken, Gobán immediately took the chest home and set about making it a little bit higher. Then, on the occasion of the next full moon, he returned to the market at Swords with his new and improved wooden chest, still hopeful of a trade. But it wasn't to be. Much to his surprise, the negative comments kept coming.

The first man to approach him on that particular day was a blacksmith from Feltrim. Puffing up his chest, the blacksmith declared: 'It's a fine chest to be sure, Gobán, and sure no one could have made it but yourself. But it's a little too narrow'. So Gobán took the chest home and made it a bit wider.

At the next full moon, Gobán headed off to the market and displayed the chest again. And once again, the chest attracted great attention. On this occasion, a woman's voice rose above the murmuring crowd.

'A fine chest it is to be sure, Gobán,' she remarked, 'and no one could have made it but yourself. But it is far too large to be useful and the legs are much too long.'

The crowd nodded in agreement.

Once again Gobán left the market feeling more than a little crestfallen. He took the chest home and, the following day when he had gotten over his disappointment, he proceeded to shorten the legs.

On the following market day, an even larger crowd gathered to examine the famous chest with no nails. But the first man to speak on that cold and misty morning wondered what had happened to the legs.

'It is a fine chest indeed, Gobán,' he declared, 'but why on earth did you shorten the legs? They were fine as they were, and now they are too short.'

In a rage of frustration, Gobán cracked his whip at the ox and drove angrily home.

'Back so soon?' his mother enquired. 'And in such a foul temper. What wild storm is raging inside that head of yours now?'

'Nobody likes the chest,' sighed Gobán. 'I just can't seem to please anyone.'

'Oh, I doubt that,' said his mother. 'I think what you mean to say is that you are finding it impossible to please *everyone*. Is that not so?'

Gobán nodded.

'Well then,' said his mother, 'perhaps you have learnt one of the most important lessons that life has to teach us – that, however hard you try, you cannot please everyone. Perhaps the time you've spent making and altering that enormous chest has not been wasted after all.'

Gobán nodded silently. Never again would he try to please everyone. He would trust himself and do what *he* thought was right, no matter what others might think. With that in mind, the very next day he removed the legs from the chest and put it to use as a toolbox. And it was as well that he did, for in the years to come that giant chest would play a big part in the saving of his life.

THE CAT WITH
TWO TAILS

AS GOBÁN GREW to manhood, he slowly
progressed from making boxes and tables to
building bridges, houses, and barns. But unlike
his father, who had always built circular wooden
huts according to the old traditions, Gobán began
to build both circular and rectangular buildings,
and with a mixture of both wood *and* stone.

His skill was quickly recognised, not least by
himself, and gradually he lost the modesty of his
youth. His fame grew almost as quickly as his
pride and he worked harder and harder to better
himself. In no time at all, there was not a single

craftsman that was his equal in all of Ireland, or one that was more sought after.

But Gobán did not just design these new kinds of houses, he helped to build them as well. Without ever having to be taught, he mastered no less than sixteen trades and became the most skilled stonemason that Ireland had ever seen. The forts and stone walls he built were said to be almost impenetrable, and the houses free from damp and draughts, famous for the sturdiness of their walls and the tightness of their thatch.

As his reputation spread, people stopped calling him 'Gobán, son of Tuirbe', and began to give him a name in his own right. Throughout the length and breadth of Ireland, he became known as *Gobán Saor*, or Gobán the Builder.

A steady stream of work now flowed his way, and his family prospered. Their house became as comfortable as a king's and their table laden with such princely treats as butter, yoghurt, honey, and mead. But Gobán wasn't satisfied with comfort. He was still a young man. He wanted to travel and see a little of the world before he settled down.

It is good to get away from home sometimes, to live without the sense that you are being constantly watched or judged. But getting away isn't always easy for celebrities, and Gobán could go nowhere but people wanted to talk to him about his work. He knew better than to reveal his trade secrets, of course, but the effort of concealing them was never less than tiresome.

No more than any other profession, the secrets of the builder were jealously guarded, for the less who knew and understood them, the more valuable they became. To protect his secrets from other builders, Gobán even invented a new language, the *Bearla Lagair*, so that he could instruct his team without fear of eavesdroppers.

His invented language would eventually become the secret language of stone-masons everywhere and, for a long time after his death, no apprentice mason would be able to qualify until he could speak it fluently.

The *Bearla Lagair* was useful in deterring eavesdroppers, but it was little defence against observation. And so, whenever Gobán travelled, he would disguise himself as a travelling workman and take any kind of work he could find. He travelled in disguise because he knew that, were his identity to become known, he would be watched like a hawk, or kidnapped and forced to work for free.

Occasionally, however, his pride would get the better of him. Indeed it came to pass that one day, while he was travelling through the county of Kildare, he chanced upon a place where some men were building a house. Being hungry, he asked if they had any work going.

'Not for the likes of you we don't,' said the master-builder. 'We don't employ tramps.'

Feeling more than a little insulted, Gobán waited until the men had left for their lunch, before returning to the site. Taking a mallet from his bag of tools, he flung it so violently at one of the roof rafters that it caused it to shift and become crooked. When the men came back from lunch, they noticed the roof had shifted and despaired of having to rebuild it.

Gobán wandered up to them. 'I could save you hours of work,' he said, 'and fix that roof in a matter of seconds. All it would cost you is a single plump hen.'

The men laughed, but agreed, more out of the prospect of some light entertainment than the belief that he could actually do it. Taking his mallet from his bag, Gobán threw it at the rafter from the opposite side, and with just the right amount of force that it moved back to its original position, and no further. The workmen's jaws dropped in astonishment.

Gobán was given his hen and offered several days' work. But if there was work enough for him now, there had been work enough before. He refused to work for those who could treat a stranger so unkindly. Without a word of thanks or explanation, he took his hen and his tool bag and set off for the next village, his heart bursting with pride in his own abilities.

Some days later, while passing through what is now the county of Tipperary, Gobán applied to the master-builder of the new monastery for work.

'What is your trade?' asked the master.

'Whatever is required,' replied Gobán somewhat arrogantly. 'Try me and see.'

The master, unconvinced by Gobán's display of self-confidence, directed him to a corner of the building site and pointed to a stone slab. 'I have need of a mason,' he said. 'Carve from that slab a cat with two tails and when I return tomorrow we'll see if your skills are a match for your confidence.'

Now Gobán, being a bit of a perfectionist, couldn't help himself, and during the night he

carved a lifelike cat with two tails out of the stone slab. A task that might have taken any other mason several days to complete, Gobán completed in a half a night and by firelight alone. When he had finished, he stood back to admire his work.

The wave of satisfaction that passed over him as he admired his creation, was quickly replaced by a flush of panic. The cat was just *too* good. No one would be able to gaze upon it without realizing who had made it.

Fearing that if his identity became known he might be kidnapped and forced to work for some greedy chieftain, he gathered his tools and fled as fast as his feet could carry him deep into the moonlit forest, where he knew that few would dare to follow.

In those days the country was covered by vast forests that were far larger than anything that exists today. If you left the known paths, the chances of anyone finding you in the event of a mishap were few. People rarely ventured into the dark interior of the forests on account of the wickedness that was widely believed to lurk there.

But Gobán was not afraid of ogres, witches, or banshees. Nor was he afraid of wolves. He was a trained hunter and knew the difference between the howl of a wolf and the call of a witch, and between the scream of a vixen and the wail of a banshee.

And that wasn't all that he knew, for his father, who had been so favoured by the gods, had also taught him how to carve a secret ogham spell into the trunk of a tree that would protect a man from wolves, fairies and wild boars. And so, even in the darkest woods, Gobán always slept peacefully.

Now it came to pass that, early the following morning, when the master-builder returned, he found the rock he had asked Gobán to carve covered with a dusty calfskin rug. Pulling it away, he discovered the most beautiful and lifelike sculpture of a cat he had ever seen – a cat, indeed, with two tails.

'Oh what a fool I've been,' he sighed disconsolately, 'for that beggar simply had to have been Gobán Saor himself. There is not another man in all of Ireland that could have done such superb work, or so quickly. What a fool I've been. I should have paid more attention to his boasting, for it was never the way of a simple beggar to be so arrogant.'

The master-builder called his workmen together and showed them the cat.

'Who made that?' they asked as one.

'Why, who else *could* have made it?' said the master-builder, 'but Gobán Saor himself. Now divide yourselves into four groups of two, and go out into those hills and find him. The chieftain will surely pay handsomely to have the finest craftsman in Ireland amongst his slaves and servants..'

Excited at the prospect of a reward, the men set out with great enthusiasm and scoured the tracks and trails that led from the village, searching high and low without success. They returned as the first glow of dawn began to seep into the sky. Each told the same story. Gobán Saor had vanished.

'Oh well,' sighed the master, 'at least we have the cat, and it has cost us nothing.'

From that day forward, to remind himself never to take excessive pride in his work, Gobán would always leave the image of a cat with two tails somewhere within his creations. And that, according to the old tales, was how the 'mason's mark' was born. Such marks would soon be used by stonemasons all over the world to sign their work, but none would ever be as elaborate as Gobán's cat.

Some of Gobán's cats have survived to this very day, especially in the area of South Tipperary, where he happened to carve his first.

If you are ever in the area, you will find the best of them situated above the entrance to the Swiss Cabin in Cahir.

GOBÁN AND RÁIMSEACH

By THE TIME Gobán had reached his early twenties his father, Tuirbe, had begun to worry about what would happen to his lands after he had died. As his only son, Gobán would, as tradition demanded, inherit everything. But the boy had little interest in hunting and farming, even though he was earning as much as four cows for every house he built. Tuirbe was a proud man. He feared that his lands, and the memory of his deeds, would be lost through his son's neglect.

Gobán, you see, would often be away for many

moons at a time, travelling with his team of stonemasons, carpenters, and thatchers, and living in simple tents covered with animal skins. It was a hard life, and whenever the team returned to Turvey they would be so exhausted that not a man amongst would have the energy to help around their family's farm.

'Our daughters are all married and caring for their husbands and their husbands' parents,' said Tuirbe to his wife one night. 'Only Gobán is left single. We will soon be too old to manage by ourselves and will need the assistance of a daughter-in-law who will care for us in our final years. It has long been a tradition amongst us that a boy's parents would select his bride.'

'And is that not as it should be?' said Dearbhail. 'Is it not better that those who care most for him would select the girl that will be best for him... and also for them?'

'Perhaps,' said Tuirbe, 'But I fear Gobán's response. He is a stubborn and independent creature. I fear he will dishonour us by refusing our choice. He no longer has any need of my lands, or indeed of my gold, and he is not given to suffering fools. He will not accept just any girl.'

'I have long feared the same,' said Dearbhail. 'If only we could find a girl that is his equal in cleverness?'

'Alas,' said Tuirbe. 'I have never met another the equal of him in that regard, either male or female.'

'This much is true,' said Dearbhail. 'In all of Brega I, too, have never once heard of such a girl.'

'Then we have little choice but to cast a wider net,' said Tuirbe. 'I am loath to do so, but I will speak to him in the morning.'

When Tuirbe told Gobán of his intentions, his son became furious. 'You will make me the laughing stock of Leinster,' he protested. 'I'm far too young to marry. I won't do it, I tell you. I just won't.'

'You would dishonour your parents?' asked

Tuirbe.

'It is not my intention,' said Gobán, 'but, when the time comes, I will choose my own bride.'

'But that's what we have been trying to tell you,' said Tuirbe. 'The time *has* come. Your mother and I are getting old and it's high time you faced up to your responsibilities.'

'Well then, said Gobán, 'if it is as you say it is, and you and mother are set on this course, then I will meet you halfway. I will accept your choice of bride, *if*, and only if, the girl can meet certain conditions.'

'And what might *they* be?' asked Tuirbe.

'Your word, first,' said Gobán. 'I want your word of honour that you will accept them. Otherwise, I shall leave this place forever and make my own way in the world.'

'This is a sad state of affairs,' sighed Tuirbe, 'but I am already an old man. You leave me no choice but to accept.'

'I shall make it simple for you,' said Gobán.

'The girl must come to Ráth Tuirbhí without coming in the day or in the night, without walking on the tracks or in the fields, and she must come by herself but not alone.'

Tuirbe was stunned, but he had given his word. He walked away, his head bowed, wondering how he was going to tell his wife that he had been tricked.

But then, the following spring, as the winds began to blow mild and the whitethorn to blossom, a footsore and weary young woman arrived unannounced at Ráth Tuirbhí. She was a pretty girl, with golden hair more radiant than the setting sun and a voice sweeter than song. She knocked on the doorpost of their house just as Tuirbe and Gobán were finishing a game of *fidchell*, the ancient Irish form of chess.

'Good health to all here,' she called confidently. 'I come in search of the family of Gobán Saor, son of Tuirbe of the Strands.'

'You are welcome here kind stranger,' said

Tuirbe, staring at her dark rags and mud-encrusted feet and trying to make out her facial features through the smoke of a freshly lit fire. From the state of her clothes, it was obvious that she had been travelling for some time. 'I am Tuirbe. Have you come far?'

'From Dowth,' she answered. 'My late parents were of the Uí Néill, the finest and richest family in Ireland. But I am mistress of my own fate now and will not be tied to some *amadán* for the sake of a political alliance. A certain riddle has the whole country intrigued. I have come to meet its creator.'

'Do you have a name child?' asked Gobán's mother.

'I am called Ráimseach,' said the girl. 'Ráimseach Ruadh, on account of my hair. They say I have a temper to match, but it is only a fool who would test the truth of it.'

The girl was slender, pretty, and as noble in her bearing as one might expect from the daughter of an Uí Néill. And she had a great deal to say for herself, but in a self-confident rather than an arrogant way.

Ráimseach had been looking at Gobán's parents as she spoke, but as Gobán shifted on his bench, she turned for the first time to face him. Startled by her beauty, a flush of heat rose in his cheeks.

'You… you know my terms?' he stuttered.

'I do indeed,' said Ráimseach.

'Pray tell, then,' said Gobán, 'how in the name of all the gods you managed to meet them.'

'Well,' said Ráimseach, 'you said not to come in the day nor in the night, so I travelled only at dusk and at dawn. You said not to come by the tracks nor the fields, so I travelled by ditches, rivers, and sea.'

'You have done well,' said Gobán, 'but there was a third condition.'

'To come by myself, but not alone?'

'Exactly, and yet here you are. I see no other

person.'

'Nor is there,' said Ráimseach, 'and yet I am not alone.'

She opened her cloak, revealing an apron with a deep pocket. She bid Gobán come forth and examine it and, as he came within a pace of her, she pulled it towards him revealing a sleeping puppy.

'I am beaten,' laughed Gobán. 'Trapped by my own words. Come join us by the fire. You must be hungry.'

The following day, just to be certain that Ráimseach Ruadh was more than just a clever girl with a pretty face and fine golden hair, Tuirbe handed her a heavily knotted ball of yellow thread that was so tangled it appeared almost impossible to unravel.

'Our old eyes are not what they were,' he said. 'Would you be so kind as to untangle this? It is the last we have in this colour and it is needed to repair my wife's favourite cloak.'

Ráimseach took the ball of thread and retired to a quiet corner to attempt to unravel it. She stayed at her task, both day and night, until she had untangled every single knot. Her persistence impressed Tuirbe. 'This indeed is the woman to whom our son will be married,' he proclaimed loudly. And do you know what, just thirty sunrises later they were.

Over the years that followed, Ráimseach proved to be Gobán's equal in almost everything. She could handle an axe and a sword as skilfully as any man, and would even accompany her husband on his building projects and carry stones to him in her apron. She also gave birth to his children.

It was shortly after the birth of his fifth daughter, that Gobán's parents died. His mother went first, during a severe winter. Shortly afterwards, unwilling to endure the pain of separation, his father took his spear and his famous axe, slipped quietly from the ring fort one melancholy evening, and disappeared deep into the woods.

His body was found later that summer by a shepherd boy, lying by the side of a stream, his back propped against the mossy side of a hazel tree, his wife's cloak wrapped about his shoulders. His spear lay by his side, his axe hung from his leather belt, and beneath his unclosed eyes, the tracks of tears were visible on his face.

As there were no visible wounds on his body and it appeared to be little more than skin and bone, the assumption was made that he had died of a broken heart, his grief having driven him to starvation in an attempt to speed his reunion with Dearbhail in the otherworld.

In accordance with his wishes, Tuirbe and his axe were buried in Portrane, at a place that would come to be called *Tuladh an Bhiail* or the 'Hill of the Axe', with Tuirbe's head resting on a rock pillow facing out to sea. The enchanted axe would never again be thrown.

The death of Gobán's parents meant that, during his many absences, Ráimseach would now be left to manage the farm alone. And she was quite able, in most respects. But not in ploughing. She simply could not control the oxen. They did not like her, and she did not like them.

There was a field on a hill close to the estuary that had been recently cleared of gorse. Ráimseach wanted it ploughed so that she might sow barley and turnips. For seven long years, she had been pestering Gobán to plough that field for her. But every time she asked, the answer was always the same.

'I'm designing a new plough that will do the work in half the time,' he'd say. 'I'll do it when I'm finished. There's no rush. We can always trade cattle for turnips and barley.'

'We can at that,' said Ráimseach, 'but I want to live like everyone else, to be with the other women and enjoy my food all the more for having grown it myself. It is how it should be, and how it has always been.'

Between one thing and another, the field was never ploughed. But then one year, in the early spring, Gobán finally finished his new plough. Harnessing the oxen, he ploughed from dawn until dusk, returning that evening dreadfully pleased with himself for having ploughed a field in one day that used to take three.

'All done,' he boasted gleefully, 'and in record time.'

'Record time, is it?' laughed Ráimseach. 'Sure it's only taken you seven years!'

That same autumn, after the wheat had been harvested, the annual forage for nuts and berries completed, and the acorns boiled, leached and ground into flour, Ráimseach found herself alone in the woods, chopping wood for the winter fires.

This was normally Gobán's job, but Gobán and his team had set out for a job in Naul and the farmhand had gone to the emporium on Lambay to trade a calf-skin for some Saxon pottery.

Unwilling to wait, Ráimseach decided to chop the wood herself. Alas, the axe that Gobán had left her was too blunt to bring down a mature tree. It was only good for chopping small branches. But even these were hard work. She searched for a sharper axe, without success, but managed to find a mallet and an iron wedge. Desperate for firewood, she attempted to improvise.

Selecting a young tree, Ráimseach used the pointed corner of the blunted axe to create a nick in the trunk large enough to take the tip of the wedge, then hammered the wedge with her mallet until a crack opened in the trunk. For almost an hour the blows of her mallet echoed through the woods until, with a loud splintering snap, a split raced halfway up and down the trunk.

With a little more work, she thought, the trunk would split entirely, and she might be able to put her back to each half and push it to the ground. The blunt axe could then be used to chop off the smaller branches that had previously been out of her reach.

Gobán and his men, in the meantime, had only got as far as Ballyboughal before they were waylaid by bandits. His companions were killed, but Gobán himself was recognised and spared. The bandits took him back to Ráth Tuirbhí intent on forcing him to hand over his riches. The fort at Ráth Tuirbhí was empty when they arrived, and Gobán was adamant in his refusal to hand over his gold. Hearing a woman singing in the woods, the bandits left Gobán with a guard and went to find her.

'Stop what you are doing,' said their leader as he closed on Ráimseach, 'We have killed all of your husband's men and we will kill him too unless you hand over his gold.'

'Where is Gobán now?' asked Ráimseach. 'How do I know he is not already dead?'

'He is back at your house, tied up and guarded.

Now do as we say, or he will surely die this day.'

'I will lead you to his gold,' said Ráimseach coolly, 'when I have retrieved this metal wedge from the tree. You can help, or you can wait. It's all the same to me.'

Impatient to get their hands on Gobán's gold, the bandits decided to help. Placing their fingers in the crack, they attempted to pull the two sides of the tree far enough apart to allow the wedge to be taken out. No sooner were their finger inside the crack, however, than Ráimseach hit the wedge with the mallet from below, sending it flying into the sky.

The two sides of the tree that had been separated by the wedge now sprang back into place, trapping the men by their fingers. As they struggled to free themselves, Ráimseach swung her mallet and bashed in their heads.

Returning to the house, Ráimseach told the man guarding Gobán that she had paid the ransom and his colleagues had left. Convinced he was being cheated, the remained bandit fled the house in search of them and was never seen again. That night, Gobán said a prayer of thanks to the goddess Danu, mother of all the gods, for having sent him so brave and clever a wife. 'I have been blessed,' he told himself, 'truly, truly blessed.'

GOBÁN AND THE YEW OF ROSS

A LONG, LONG time ago, before people learned to read and write, when history was told as fireside entertainment and people still believed in the old gods, a giant strolled into the great enclosure on the Hill of Tara.

Everyone stopped what they were doing and stared. The giant's shoulders were as high as the treetops, and his waist was so high that the sky could be seen between his legs. He had long golden hair that shone as bright as a furnace and wore sandals that were made from a mysterious material no one had ever seen before.

The giant's name was Trefuilngid Tre-eochair – the Celtic god of wisdom. Fearing that the people were losing faith in the old gods, he had taken the form of a giant and descended to earth, bringing nothing with him but a leafy branch that bore three different kinds of fruit: nuts, apples, and acorns. There wasn't a tree on earth that could do that.

It was obvious that Trefuilngid was not of this world, and that whatever he requested would have to be done. So, when he asked the High King to command the seven wisest men in Ireland to come to Tara, it was duly done. One did not quibble with a god.

Over the course of the following year, Trefuilngid taught the wise men all about their origins and their heritage, and shared with them his vast knowledge of the universe and the otherworld. Before he left, he turned to an old greybeard called Fintan.

'Here, old man,' he said. 'Take these fruits from

the sacred tree of the otherworld and plant one in each of the five provinces. The trees that grow from them will protect you from evil for as long as they live.'

Ah now, I can hear you saying, there are only four provinces in Ireland, and you are, of course, correct. But back then there was a fifth, called *Mide*. It was where the Hill of Tara was situated and where the High King of Ireland had his home. It lay roughly where the counties of Meath and Westmeath sit today and is why Meath is sometimes called 'The Royal County'.

After the giant had gone, Fintan extracted the seeds from the fruits and set about planting one in each of the five provinces as the god had directed. The trees that grew from each of these seeds became known as the five sacred trees of Ireland. The first tree that was planted was called the *Eó Rossa*, or 'Yew of Ross', and Fintan had planted it on the banks of the River Barrow in County Carlow.

Now, the yew is a special tree that can live for up to 900 years. It lives so long that the ancient Irish thought it never died. Indeed, so revered was the yew, that heavy penalties were imposed upon any man caught cutting one down. But while no human would dare to cut down a yew, the same was not true of the wind and, one day, many centuries after they had been planted, all five of the sacred trees were uprooted in a single night by a powerful storm.

At that time there happened to be living close to the Yew of Ross, a Christian abbot who went by the name of Moling. Fearful that fragments of the tree might be taken and used to encourage a revival of the old religion, Moling took possession of it and asked Gobán to build a small chapel for him on the site, using wood from the fallen tree. The holy site of the old gods would thus, Moling hoped, become a holy site of the new.

Gobán's father would never have taken such a job, but Gobán had no such qualms. The tree had already fallen and it was not, in any case, against the ancient laws to use a *fallen* yew. And so Gobán set out for Carlow, taking with him two workers, their wives, and his wife, Ráimseach.

On reaching Carlow, Gobán and his team were joined by Moling, who was himself a carpenter, and together they set about stripping the smaller branches from the yew. As they worked, a splinter of wood hit Moling in the eye, temporarily blinding him.

Unwilling to see the work stop, Moling hid his injury, pulled the hood of his dark brown habit over his face, and retired to a corner of the site to read the bible with his one good eye. No sooner had he started reading than the sight returned to his injured eye.

'A miracle,' he mumbled to himself, convinced that it was a sign from God.

During the building of the chapel, there came a day when all the men were needed on-site and none were free to stand guard over the cattle. So it fell to the women to bring the two milking cows that Moling had provided to the river to drink. The women were Ráimseach, Brigid and Gráinne. It was a very hot day and, as the cattle drank, the women sought shelter in the shade of a tree.

'This heat is unbearable,' said Gráinne. 'I feel like I'm going to melt.'

'Let's go for a swim,' said Brigid excitedly.

'We can't,' said Gráinne. 'We can't leave the cows unguarded.'

'Oh, the cows will be fine,' said Brigid. 'They're cows, after all. They won't go far. Come on Ráimseach, tell her. It'll be fine.'

'Oh, alright then,' said Ráimseach. 'Just a quick dip to cool off. I don't suppose there's any harm in that.'

The women undressed, left their clothes in three neat piles, and waded into the river. The current was too strong for swimming, but they were happy enough to wade in the shallows close to the bank. All that mattered was that the water was cool and refreshing.

Noticing that the cows had been left unprotected, a local thief by the name of Grac crept out of the woods and made off with one of them. Seeing him flee, the women screamed for the men, but they could not be heard above the noise of their hammering. It fell to Ráimseach to tell Moling what had happened.

'The thief can only be Grac,' said Moling, 'for no one else in these parts would dare to steal from me. I'll send some of the brothers after him. They will teach the brute such a lesson that no one will dare to bother you again.'

The monks overtook Grac just as the sun was setting. He was camped by the side of the river and had already killed and skinned the cow. The beast was already roasting on a spit over an open fire as the monks arrived.

When Grac saw the monks approaching he climbed a nearby tree, intending to hide from them. But the tree, alas, was covered in a damp moss that was so greasy that it caused him to slip and fall into the fire.

With his clothes aflame, Grac ran for the river and dived in. Between the severity of his burns and the strength of the current, he struggled to swim. Within minutes the poor thief had drowned.

The monks quickly put out the fire, took the roasting cow from the spit, and wrapped it in its hide. They then proceeded to carry the half-cooked beast back to Moling. On receiving the beast, Moling blessed it with holy water and miraculously restored it to life.

Or at least that was the story that the monks told Grac's family, and everyone else who would listen to them, in order to convince them of Moling's great magic, just in case anyone might be thinking of avenging the death of Grac.

But Moling wasn't finished yet. To teach the builders to take better care of the cattle they had been entrusted with, Moling refused to replace the stolen cow, forcing Ráimseach to give Gobán an ultimatum.

'One cow will not produce enough milk to feed all of us,' she protested. 'If you don't fix this quickly, the women will have to leave.'

Gobán was furious. He immediately went to Moling and demanded that he be given another milking cow to replace the one that had been stolen.

'Even if I wanted to,' countered Moling. 'Such a thing would be impossible. We would not be able to get another milker for you at this time of year and there is no longer a person for miles around who will dare to loan you one for fear that it, too, will be lost.'

'Then you had better find another source of food for my team,' said Gobán, 'and find it fast. For I tell you now, priest, that chapel will remain unfinished until the floor of it has been covered with sacks of oats. I will not allow my men to starve.'

'That is far more than what we agreed,' sighed Moling, 'and a price that will cause great hardship to my fellow monks come winter.'

'And what about my men?' Gobán thundered. 'Do you expect *them* to work on empty stomachs? You will fill the chapel, or we are leaving. It's up to you.'

'I'll see what I can do,' growled Moling as he tramped off towards the village.

'Why did you ask for so much grain?' asked Ráimseach after Moling had gone. 'It is far more than we will need.'

'Because he was being disrespectful,' said Gobán. 'I wanted to teach him a lesson.'

'I doubt you will get any more respect from him by being greedy,' said Ráimseach.

'Perhaps not,' said Gobán, 'but he'll think twice about cheating his workers in future.'

Moling, meanwhile, was struggling to gather enough grain to meet Gobán's demands and, in desperation, he had to resort to padding out the sacks with nuts and apples. One way or another, he managed to fill six of the required number of sacks, but it was a risky strategy. He had no idea what might happen when his trick was discovered. He could only pray that the building work would be finished before it was.

The following morning, when the workers arrived on site, they found the chapel filled with what they took to be sacks of grain.

'Check them,' said Gobán. 'and make sure it is grain and not sand that is in them.'

The workers opened a few sacks at random, but as the heavier apples and nuts had by now settled on the bottom, even if the opened sacks had been those that had been padded out with fruit and nuts, all that would have been seen was oats and barley.

'My brothers will go hungry this winter,' groaned Moling, 'but mark my words Gobán, we shall soon see which is greater, the power of God or the greed of Gobán Saor.'

Ignoring Moling's threats, Gobán and his team set about finishing the chapel, during which time the apples inside the six padded sacks began to rot. When the work was finished, they loaded the remaining unopened sacks onto their pack horses and set out for home.

They had travelled but a single day's journey, however, when they happened to open the first of the six padded sacks, hoping to make some porridge. Alas, it was not oats that they found inside, but a swarm of maggots and fruit flies. Every other sack bar one was the same. Very little of the grain was edible.

'Serves you right,' scolded Ráimseach. 'I told you that no good would come from greed. Now let that be a lesson to you. The women alone will eat from the good sack and you and your team will ride out first thing in the morning and try to find someone who will sell you some oats. I'll warrant, however, that news of your treatment of Moling will have travelled before you and you will search long for a man who will sell to you at a fair price. Every action has its consequences, Gobán, every last one of them.'

THE BOASTFUL SCOTSMAN

A SCOTTISH MERCHANT by the name of Allistor Bruce, once married an Irishwoman by the name of Ailbe O'Connor. In need of a larger house for his growing family, he hired Gobán to build one close to where the Poddle flowed into River Liffey.

Ireland was still a wild and heavily forested place at this time and roads were few and far between. Goods were sent most quickly by rivers or by sea, so it was important for a merchant to live beside a river. The Scotsman had already bought a plot of land close to the Liffey and he promised to pay Gobán handsomely if he would construct a house for him close to the banks, but it had to be a fine house, one befitting a man of such great wealth.

Gobán agreed to take on the job. But the building had no sooner started than the Scotsman became something of a pest, turning up at the most awkward of times and forever boasting about how wealthy he was. Gobán quickly tired of Bruce's self-importance and did his best to avoid him. But one day, as the house was nearing completion, Gobán was delayed on-site and Bruce happened to arrive before he could get away.

'Come with me Gobán,' said the Scotsman, 'and let me treat you to a fine meal. You would be doing me the greatest honour, for I have more gold than I know what to do with and few friends with whom to share it.'

Taking pity on the man, Gobán went with him to a local inn, where they enjoyed a fine meal. He couldn't help but notice, however, when the meal was finished, that Bruce had paid for it with ten small silver coins, a form of payment that was rare enough at the time in a country with no currency.

'You must allow me to return the favour,' said Gobán. 'Allow *me* to treat *you* to a meal tomorrow.'

'I'll not hear a word of it,' said the Scotsman. I can't have you wasting the silver I've paid you on me. It would not be right.'

'Sir,' said Gobán. 'I work as a builder because it pleases me to see things built and hear people say that it was Gobán himself who built them. But I have little need of silver because some years ago I built a house for an old witch who paid me with two very special gifts.'

Reaching into his satchel, Gobán pulled out a white woollen cap.

'This,' he said, 'is one of them. The other is with my wife. They are wishing caps and they provide me with the power of persuasion. As long as we have them my family wants for nothing, for there is always someone who can be persuaded to provide what we need.'

'Forgive me,' said the Scotsman, 'if I find that hard to believe. This is a joke, no?'

'Your doubts are understandable,' retorted Gobán, pretending to hurt pride. 'But I am an artisan, not a jester. I do not play jokes. If you will allow me to take you to dinner tomorrow, I will prove the truth of it.'

There were but three alehouses in Dublin at that time, for the town was made up of little more than a few clusters of homes that had been built around the monasteries or close to the moorings where the ships would lay up. Late that night, under cover of darkness, Gobán called to them all. He gave each innkeeper ten small pieces of silver and told them what he wanted them to do. The following day, when Bruce came calling, Gobán was ready and waiting for him.

'Ah, good,' said Gobán. 'You came! Seeing as I shall be paying for the meal, perhaps you would like to choose the inn. It makes little difference to me where we eat.'

The Scotsman chose the same inn as they had been to the previous day, and just as he had done on the last occasion on which they had dined together, Bruce presumed to order for them both. As she turned to leave, Gobán caught hold of the innkeeper's wife by the arm.

'By the power of this cap,' he said, slapping his woollen cap on the table, 'I shall have those meals and the price of both.'

The Scotsman looked puzzled, but said nothing. But, when the meals were eventually served, the innkeeper's wife not only put a plate of food in front of Gobán, she also presented him with but ten tiny pieces of silver, which was the price of their meal.

'You can keep the silver,' said Gobán, 'as payment.'

The Scotsman waited until the innkeeper's wife had left, then leaned across the table. 'Why did you do that?' he asked. 'Why did you wish for the silver when you could have simply wished for a free meal?'

'Ah,' said Gobán. 'Because I am an honourable man. I will not have it said that I never paid for what I have eaten.'

'You truly *are* a strange creature,' said Bruce. 'But I have enjoyed your company and would like to see more of this cap. Shall we dine again tomorrow?'

'I have no objection,' said Gobán, 'but perhaps we should go somewhere else. We have imposed on this family enough.'

Over the next two days, at the other two alehouses, the same play was carried out for the Scotsman's benefit. With each and every meal, the Scotsman's desire to have Gobán's cap grew stronger and stronger.

And so it came to pass that, on the day that

Gobán completed the building and was making his preparations to leave, the Scotsman finally gave voice to his desire.

'Here is the remainder of the silver we agreed for the building of the house,' said Bruce. 'But, before you leave, I have a proposition for you. I would really like to buy that magic cap of yours. Just name your price. I am a rich man, as you know, and you have already told me that you have another just like it at home. Surely you would not miss one of them.'

'That is certainly true,' said Gobán, 'but I could not let it go. What if I were to lose the other one, or it was to be destroyed somehow? It would have to be a mighty fine price for me to even consider parting with it.'

'Would ten cows convince you?' said Bruce.

'Indeed it would not,' said Gobán, 'Indeed I would not part with it for twenty.'

'Well then,' said Bruce, 'perhaps then you would take thirty.'

Gobán paused, pretending to think long and hard.

'You have treated me well here,' said Gobán, 'and you appear to be a kind and fair man who will not misuse the cap. I doubt even the cap could convince a man to give me thirty cattle. I will accept your offer.'

And so it was that Gobán finally put a stop to the Scotsman's boasting, for when Bruce discovered that he had bought nothing more than an ordinary woollen cap, he was far too embarrassed to protest, lest he gain the reputation of a fool.

When Gobán arrived home and told Ráimseach how he had come by a herd of cows, she laughed heartily.

'You rogue,' said she. 'I wish I could have seen his face when the cap didn't work! But I've said it once, Gobán, and I'll say it again. Nothing good ever comes from greed. And speaking of greed, have you thought about where you are going to put those cows? We have barely enough pasture for the twenty we have, let alone thirty more!'

THE SECRET DAUGHTER

AFTER THE BIRTH of his sixth daughter, Gobán began to despair of ever having a son and to fear that he would be the last in his line. It weighed heavily on his pride and, though she could sense his despair, there was little that Ráimseach could do to comfort him. Such things, after all, were in the hands of the gods.

With no son to pass his land to, Gobán feared for the ability of his wife to hold onto it, and for the war that would inevitably arise between his daughters' husbands for the right to claim it as their own. But while Gobán despaired,

Ráimseach never lost hope and, when she became pregnant with her seventh child, she began to pray every single night to the goddess Brigid to let it be a boy. She had never been much of a one for prayer in the past, but desperate times called for desperate measures, and if increased devotion was what Brigid demanded, then – for the sake and love of her husband – increased devotion was what she would have.

Now it came to pass late into Ráimseach's pregnancy, that Gobán was offered a big job in Connaught that would keep him away for at least two moons. With her daughters too young to be of much assistance at the birth of a child, Ráimseach sent them to stay with their aunts and invited her oldest friend to come and stay with her. Her name was Fiadh and she, too, was with child.

'Listen Fiadh,' said Ráimseach one day. 'You have four sons and no daughters, and I have six daughters and no sons. If you give birth to a son, and I to a girl, let us swap children. It will free me of the shame of not having produced an heir, and you will finally have another female about the house.'

'Oh, Ráimseach,' said Fiadh, 'You have no idea how long my husband and I have yearned for a daughter, but Suibhne would never allow it. And, in any case, how could we possibly carry off such a great deception?'

'Our husbands,' said Ráimseach, 'would never notice and, as you will give birth first, all we would have to do is pretend that you have a fever to keep people away until I have delivered my own child. If I should then give birth to a son, nothing will be lost and no one need ever know of our agreement.'

The deal was struck and when the babies were born, Fiadh swapped her son for Ráimseach's daughter and, when their husbands returned, they found their wives nursing the object of their respective hearts' desire, Ráimseach her new son, Colmán, and Fiadh her new daughter, Liadin.

As the years flew by, the two women did their utmost to avoid each other, lest the sight of their natural children cause them sorrow or distress. Eventually, they lost touch completely and, though each raised and loved their adopted child as their own, they never forgot their natural children, nor did they ever lose hope of seeing them again.

Never was a child more loved by his parents than Colmán, and he grew up to be a fine young man. He was diligent in his work and loyal and obedient to a fault. He worked alongside Gobán without reluctance or complaint and was a great help to Ráimseach in the more physical of her domestic labours.

But though he was loved by his father, Colmán was far from admired by him, for he was not as bright as his famous parents and struggled to understand the skills that Gobán wished to pass on to him. People were generally surprised to find that the son of two highly intelligent people could be so average, but as Colmán was kind and generous they never judged him harshly for it.

'He is just like my father', Ráimseach would answer whenever questions were asked about the boy's looks or his intelligence, and since no one had ever met Ráimseach's father, and the man was long since dead, she was generally taken at her word. After all, natural gifts were often known to skip a generation.

One day, on the eve of the feast of Bealtaine, Gobán told his son, who had just reached his twentieth birthday, to go to Portrane for a sack of oats. Their winter stock was running low and the new crop was not yet harvested.

There were still some oats for sale in Portrane, but Colmán would not buy them as he thought them too expensive. The following day, his father sent him to Lusk on the same errand. But once again he came home empty-handed.

'The oats,' said Colmán, 'were even more expensive in Lusk.'

With everyone looking for oats, those who had a surplus continued to raise the price. But Colmán still refused to pay any more than he had always paid and, by the following day, there were no longer any oats to be had in all of Fingal.

'Let that be a lesson to you,' said Gobán. 'You cannot eat silver. Sometimes you simply have to pay the asking price. But don't worry, son, we'll get by. If we kill one of the cows, we can salt the meat and use the oats we save from its feed for our porridge.'

'If you wanted me to pay the asking price,' said Colmán angrily, 'why didn't you just tell me to pay it.'

'Perhaps I should have,' said his father. 'But the hardest lesson is best remembered. If you cannot work these things out for yourself, people will always try to take advantage of you. In fact, your mother and I were thinking that maybe it's time you took a wife to guide you. We will discuss it further tonight.'

Gobán and Ráimseach talked long into the early hours about finding a wife for Colmán, a conversation that had the unexpected effect of putting Ráimseach in mind of the daughter she had given away. Her head became dizzy with questions. Was Liadin married? Was she happy? Where was she living?

In no time at all Ráimseach's thoughts began to turn to the possibility of arranging a marriage between Liadin and Colmán, and by such means secretly reuniting herself with her lost daughter. She would need all her wits to do so, but she decided it was worth a try.

The following day she came to Gobán with a plan. 'Gobán,' she said, 'if we are to choose a wife for Colmán, it will have to be someone clever. I would like you to set for this girl the sort of riddle you once set for me. A riddle that only the cleverest of girls could solve.'

And so it came to pass, that on the next market day, Gobán commanded his son to bring a sheepskin to the fair at Swords. 'If any woman should ask what you want for it,' he said, 'you are to say that you want the skin *and* the price of it'.

It was a clever riddle, but a cruel one, for every time Colmán named his price he was laughed at. Nobody was going to pay him for a skin they couldn't keep! Word spread so quickly that even women who had no intention of buying began to approach him, just to see if the strange tale they had been told was actually true.

This went on for several weeks. Every day that Colmán would set out with his sheepskin, he left knowing that no sane person would ever give him the price he had asked for and then give him back the skin he'd just sold them. He hated his father for forcing him to do this but feared to disobey him.

But then, one day, just as he was about to

leave, a red-haired girl rose from the spot where the women usually sat embroidering their cloaks and approached him.

'Come with me,' she commanded, taking him by the hand. 'I'll give you your price. But you must come to my parent's cabin first.'

The young girl was so pretty and spoke so much like his mother, that Colmán obeyed her without question. Taking his hand, she pulled him over the fields, walking without speaking. When they got to her cabin, they found it deserted.

'Are your parents away,' asked Colmán.

'My mother is dead these last seven years and my father is still at the fair,' said the girl. 'Come inside and sit. This will take a while.'

'What will?'

'I'm going to clip the sheepskin and remove the wool. Then I'll give you back the skin and a hen for the wool. The skin itself is worth nothing to me.'

'I never thought of that,' said Colmán. 'You're clever to have done so. As clever, I think, as my mother. You might know her, her name is...'

'I know who she is,' said the girl. '*Everybody* in these parts knows who your parents are.'

'Then you have the advantage over me,' said Colmán.

'My name is Liadin,' said the girl. 'Liadin Ruadh, daughter of Suibhne.'

When Colmán returned home to Ráth Tuirbhí that night and presented his parents with the skin, the hen, and the story of the girl, they were both intrigued.

'Describe her to me,' said Ráimseach.

'She was pretty,' said Colmán, 'and had the finest red hair I have ever seen.'

Ráimseach's heart leapt in her chest. 'Did you catch her name?' she probed.

'Liadin Ruadh,' said her son. 'Daughter of Suibhne the mason.'

'Sure I know her father well,' exclaimed

Gobán, failing to notice the tears that were welling in his wife's eyes. 'And believe it or not, that girl was born in this very house. Tell me, are her parents living still?'

'Her father is,' said Colmán. 'Her mother died of a fever seven years past.'

Gobán turned to his wife and seeing her tears assumed them to be for the death of her old friend. He had never understood why two women who had once been so close had allowed themselves to drift apart.

'That was a clever girl,' sniffed Ráimseach. 'Perhaps even the kind that could make you happy.'

'Well now,' her husband interrupted, 'Let's not tempt fate. We do things differently in this family, and what was done for me, must be done for you.'

'True, true,' said Ráimseach. 'Solving one riddle does not make a girl clever. We'll need to see her for ourselves.'

Gobán turned to his son.

'Listen,' said he. 'Tomorrow I want you to take word to her father. Tell him to bring the girl here on the first morning that follows the next full moon. And tell him that it is our wish that she come neither dressed nor undressed.'

'But that's impossible,' protested Colmán, 'and I won't do it. I've had my fill of being made fun of. You can do it yourself this time. Let them laugh at you for a change.'

'Do as your father bids,' commanded Ráimseach. 'If the girl is all I believe her to be, she will understand what has to be done. You must trust me in this, my son, even if you do not understand it. Your parents have your best interests at heart.'

When Colmán went to the girl's cabin he found the father and daughter sowing vegetables. He relayed his father's request to old Suibhne, and the man laughed out loud, just as he expected he would.

'So, it's true what they say,' said Suibhne. 'The great Gobán Saor has a fool for a son.'

'Let him be,' Liadin cut in. 'For 'tis you who will be taken for the fool if you send him away.' Turning to Colmán she then said, 'Tell your father I'll be there'.

The morning after the next full moon, Ráimseach woke her son before daybreak.

'Get up sleepy head,' she said, 'and get yourself down to the river and wash.'

'Wash?' said Colmán drowsily. 'What for? I washed only last week.'

'Because today's the day,' said his mother. 'Aren't you excited?'

'What day?' grumbled Colmán, turning away from his mother and pulling the blankets over his head.

'That girl,' said his mother. 'Liadin. She's coming today.'

'WHAT?'

'Today,' Ráimseach repeated. 'Now make

yourself decent. Come on, get up.'

'They may not come,' sighed the son, 'given the conditions you set the poor girl.'

'She'll come,' said his mother confidently. 'She'll come.'

When Liadin arrived at Ráth Tuirbhí, she came much as her natural mother had once done. Wearing only one shoe and one glove, so that she was neither dressed nor undressed, she strode confidently on the arm of her father.

When Gobán finally set eyes on Liadin he was struck dumb with surprise. Indeed, for one brief moment, he felt as if he had been cast back in time, for Liadin, you see, was the spitting image of his wife when she had first come to Ráth Tuirbhí.

For a moment he was stuck for words. Struggling to conceal the thousand disordered thoughts that were racing through his head, he proceeded to take the girl by the hand and lead her to a strongbox in the corner of the house. As he lifted the lid, the girl's eye's widened with surprise, for in that box were hundreds of gold collars, rings, arm bracelets, and nuggets.

'Well then,' asked Gobán. 'What do you think of that? One day, hopefully not too soon, all of this will belong to my son.'

'It's alright,' said Liadin.

'Alright!' Gobán exclaimed. 'Well, you must be a queen in disguise, for 'tis a fortune to me.'

'As it is to me, sir,' said Liadin, 'and I don't doubt that it was a long time in the making. Indeed, I shall look forward to adding to it.'

No words could have sounded sweeter to Gobán's ears. He knew immediately that he had found the perfect wife for his son. The two fathers looked at each other, nodded, and then took themselves outside for a walk in the woods so that they could talk privately. When finally they returned, the bargain had been struck.

Liadin, it had been agreed, would marry Colmán but only on the condition that, should she

ever have to leave Gobán's house, she could take away with her as much of the contents of the house as she could carry in three loads upon her back.

In return, Liadin would have to agree that, for as long as he lived, she would recognise Gobán, and not her husband, as the head of the household.

Liadin did not protest. She was happy with the outcome and she was more than happy to marry Colmán. He was kind and honest. She knew that he would treat her well.

Because they were still in that season that ran from the Feast of Samhain to the Feast of Bealtaine, a time the people called the 'dark half' of the year, it was decided that the marriage would not be celebrated until the Feast of Lughnasa, the most auspicious day of the year for weddings. And that, indeed, was when the wedding took place.

A druid was sent for and came all the way from

Navan to perform the ceremony, there no longer being any druids left in Fingal, where the majority of the people had embraced the new religion. As for the wedding itself, it was celebrated, as was customary in those days, on the banks of a sacred spring that has long since disappeared.

As tradition also demanded, Colmán's hands were ceremoniously tied to Liadin's that day, and the couple declared to be bound to each other for life.

The entire peninsula gathered that night for a feast so lavish that it would be remembered for a hundred years. By nightfall, Colmán was calling Liadin his *Bríd*, after the goddess Brigid, from whose name we get the word 'bride'.

'Brigid is it now?' laughed Liadin, feigning embarrassment. 'I fear it may well be the mead that is talking and not my husband, but I shall accept the blessing, for I feel strangely at home here already.'

As for the people of the peninsula, so happy were they to see the love in Ráimseach's eyes for her new daughter-in-law, that not a word was ever spoken on the subject of their extraordinary resemblance.

HOW LIADIN
BESTED GOBÁN

ONE DAY, AS Gobán and his son were returning home from a distant job of work, the weather turned bad and they were forced to seek shelter in the house of a stranger.

'Come inside kind strangers,' called the master of the house, 'and out of this cursed rain. I will see to your horses. Go dry yourselves by the fire.'

As he entered the house, Gobán found that they were not alone in seeking shelter. A traveller from one of the Ulster clans had been forced to do the same.

An older man, a neighbour of the master, was also visiting. Every now and again the master's wife, who was preparing the evening meal, would exchange a knowing look with this man and these secretive exchanges made Gobán feel immediately uneasy. He had seen such looks before. They always led to trouble.

The four men had been sitting at the hearth for about half an hour when the woman ordered her husband to go outside and pick some fennel. As he left to do so, the neighbour pulled a bundle of herbs from his pouch and handed them to the woman. Catching the scent of the leaves as they passed in front of him, Gobán shifted from his seat and placed a hand on his son's shoulder.

'The rain has stopped,' he said, 'and there is now a moon to light our way. I think we should try to get a little further in our journey before the rain that has fallen comes down from the mountains and floods the river.'

'But you are our guests,' the returning master protested. 'Will you not wait a while longer and let us serve you some food?'

'You have already served us well,' said Gobán, 'for we sought only shelter. But we are anxious to be with our family and if we can cross the river before it floods, we will save a day on our journey.'

'I understand,' said the master. 'May your journey be safe and swift.'

'Thank you,' said Gobán. 'If we leave now, we might yet make it to Cormac's bruiden.'

'That you will,' said the master. 'But

perhaps not before nightfall. Be careful.'

Cormac was a rich man who ran a type of rest house for travellers called a *bruiden*. He did so, not to make a profit, but to gain respect amongst his people, for the worth of a man was measured not just in gold, but in the extent of his hospitality.

Colmán was not happy. He did not doubt that they would be better fed by a rich man like Cormac than by this poor family, but the thought of travelling further on an empty stomach did not appeal to him. Rising to his feet, he gathered his belongings and turned to the Ulsterman.

'You are most welcome to join us,' he said, 'and share the road.'

'No thank you,' said the Ulsterman, 'I've ridden too many miles already this day and will rest here awhile. But thank you for the offer.'

The departing pair had no sooner mounted their horses than Colmán turned to his father.

'We might have been fed here,' he said.

'Indeed we might,' said Gobán. 'On the other hand, we might well have been poisoned. Did you not see the neighbour pass the woman that bunch of leaves?'

'I did,' said Colmán, 'but I paid it little heed.'

'Well then,' said Gobán, 'it's well that one of us did, for I recognised those leaves as *Moing Mhear*, a plant the Christians call 'Devil's porridge'. In my grandfather's time, they were used as a love potion.'

'A love potion,' laughed Colmán, 'for a married woman! Her poor husband.'

'It is no laughing matter,' said Gobán.

'Some plants cast longer shadows than others, and that plant is one of them.'

'Shadows?' said Colmán. 'I don't understand.'

'That plant is deadly in large doses,' said Gobán, 'and though I could not be certain that it was meant for us, I thought it better to leave before a meal was presented that we might have to refuse.'

'This plant,' said Colmán. 'Why have you withheld the knowledge of it from me for so long? This is the first I have heard of it.'

'Not all knowledge,' sighed Gobán, 'deserves to be remembered.'

The remainder of the journey passed in silence, partly from fatigue and hunger, and partly on account of Colmán's injured pride. What other knowledge, Colmán could not help but wonder, had his father been reluctant

to trust him with?

A few hours later Gobán and Colmán, reached the gate of Cormac's *bruiden* and, despite the late hour, were heartily welcomed.

'Come in, Come in!' said Cormac. 'You are most welcome, kind strangers. Attend to your horses and I'll see to it that you will have a hot meal to warm you and a place to rest your heads. Feel free to toss a fresh log on the fire.'

Cormac was as good as his word, and Gobán and his son slept soundly that night. The following morning, however, they woke to disturbing news. On joining the breakfast table, they found Cormac and his wife discussing a murder that had taken place in the rath they had left the previous evening.

'Who was it that was killed,' asked Colmán

nervously.

'The master,' said the woman of the house. 'T'was a stranger who did it. An Ulsterman, they say. He has been taken prisoner.'

'Exactly how did the master die?' Gobán now cut in.

'Poisoned,' said the woman.

'Then it was not the Ulsterman who did it,' declared Gobán, 'for I happened to witness someone else passing the *Moing Mhear* to his wife. He was a tall man. A neighbour, he said. He had a small scar above his left eyebrow.'

Armed with this information, Cormac went straight to the local *Brehon*, and the murderers were quickly arrested. Gobán and his son had to stay an extra day to give evidence, but they were soon on their way again. They did not wait to witness the fate of the murderers or the funeral of the murdered man.

When they finally reached home, the pair were so full of their own importance for having saved the Ulsterman that the tale was told and re-told many, many times. But not everyone was impressed by their behaviour.

'You pair are too clever by half,' grumbled Liadin, 'perhaps even cowards in your own way.'

'COWARDS!' thundered Gobán. 'How dare you speak to me like that.'

'What else would you call a man who believes that a murder is about to take place and yet does nothing to prevent it? Had you an ounce of your father's courage, that poor man might not have died.'

'Had we not the right to preserve our own

lives first?' protested Gobán, 'or would you rather we had eaten from the same bowl as the dead man?'

But Liadin was having none of it. Her hackles were up.

'Your own lives, is it?' said she. 'Would it have killed you to warn the Ulsterman? Or to alert the poisoners to the fact that you recognised the leaves of a deadly plant. But no, you had to prove your cleverness and save only yourselves. Words fail me!'

She was right of course, and the pair felt instantly ashamed. A silence fell upon the room that took a long time to lift, and neither father nor son ever boasted of the incident, or their part in it, again.

Following her outburst, relations between Liadin and her husband were soon mended, but her relationship with her father-in-law remained strained, injured pride being often the slowest of all wounds to heal.

In presenting Gobán with a grandson, Liadin had previously endeared herself to her father-in-law. He adored the child, and she knew it. But all of that had been soured by her accusation of cowardice.

Over the course of the following week the tension in the house continued to build until, one morning, unhappy with how Liadin was failing to discipline her son, Gobán exploded. Things were said that should never be said between members of the same family, let alone those living under the same roof, and a furious Gobán ordered Liadin to get out and never come back.

Calling on a servant as a witness, Liadin demanded that the conditions of her marriage contract be met and that she be allowed to carry her three loads from the house on her back. As this unusual condition was well known throughout the fort, Gobán had little choice but to agree.

The first of the three loads Liadin carried outside, was little Fiach, her son, whom she gave to the neighbour woman to hold for her. On her second journey, she proceeded to take as many gold nuggets from the family strong box as she could carry in her apron pocket. But it was not more gold she returned for on her third visit, rather something more precious to Gobán than life itself.

'Husband dear,' called Liadin to Colmán, who had only just that moment returned from the fields. 'Your father has told me to leave and so I am taking everything that's rightfully mine. So, if you ever want to see your son again, then you will stand on that table and ask no questions.'

Colmán did as his wife commanded, to the amusement of the curious neighbours that had by now gathered outside the house o witness the commotion.

'Now climb aboard my back,' she commanded her husband, 'and hold on tight.'

More than once her knees almost buckled under the weight of her husband but, with an almost superhuman effort, she managed to carry him outside. When Gobán saw that he was about to lose both his son and grandson, his anger cooled. He raced to the door and begged Liadin not to leave.

'I am truly sorry for all that I have said in anger,' he cried, 'and I swear by the mighty Dagda and the Holy Mother, Danu, that I will never treat you in that manner ever again. Come back, please.'

Liadin accepted Gobán's oath and went back inside, and it was just as well that she did, for in just a few years Gobán would owe his life to Liadin's bravery, and her cleverness.

THE SHORTENED ROAD

AS GOBÁN'S HAIR began to turn grey and his legs began to fail him, it became a habit of the family that someone should accompany him whenever he set out on a journey, just in case he met with an accident along the way.

It was on one such day that Gobán and his son set out for Malahide to meet a man who wanted a bridge built across a stream. It was a bitterly cold day and the pair walked side by side, shivering in silence. As they approached the shores of the Broadmeadow Estuary, Gobán turned to his son.

'Shorten the journey, can't you?' he snapped, his temper frayed by the bitter cold. 'I swear this track gets longer every year.'

Colmán began to walk faster, thinking greater speed would shorten the journey and help to warm them. But the old man couldn't keep pace with him and was soon lagging behind. Colmán waited by a fallen tree for him to catch up.

'Useless,' Gobán panted heavily. 'I asked you to shorten the road and all you have managed to do is to lengthen it. You are truly the most frustrating of companions.'

'How do you expect me to shorten the road,' Colmán protested, 'if your own two feet cannot shorten it? I can hardly be held responsible for your age.'

'In the name of all the gods,' sighed Gobán, 'how do *you* ever expect to make your fortune when you can't do a little thing like this? Go home, son. You're no use to me today. I'll manage better on my own.'

The following week they set out again on the journey – the work having been stopped by bad weather. As they made their way through the woods at Ballymadrough, Gobán again turned to his son.

'Shorten the journey, will you?' he said, 'for the cold air has pierced my bones.'

'This road is as long as ever it was,' said Colmán. 'Is it carrying over the water in a boat you're after? For I can see no shorter route and the water is too deep for us to wade across.'

'Go home,' said Gobán disappointedly. 'I'll manage better on my own.'

That night Colmán told his wife what had passed between himself and his father, and Liadin sat down to think. 'Tell me this,' she said at length. 'What did you and your father talk about on the road?'

'Why nothing at all,' said Colmán. 'Sure what would we have to talk about? There's hardly a word spoken in this house that is not heard by everyone else. What could I tell him that he has not heard already?'

'I see,' said Liadin. 'Well, silence would certainly lengthen the road, especially at his age. So the next time he asks you to shorten the road, just tell him a story. It's many the long night that was shortened at my father's hearth by an old poet, and if a story can shorten the night, it can surely shorten the road.'

The following day, when his father asked him to shorten the road, Gobán began to tell him a story that an old fisherman had once told him. The story was about a thin, swift-footed man called Caoilte Mac Ronáin, the fastest runner of the *Fianna,* a wild band of ancient warriors whose job it had once been to defend Ireland against invading armies and monsters.

Caoilte was a nephew of the great Fionn Mac Cumhaill and, along with his cousin, Oisín, was one of only two survivors of the terrible Battle of Gabhra, in which the great Fionn Mac Cumhaill lost his life fighting the forces of the High King of Ireland.

Before the *Fianna* had fallen out with the High King, some of them had been so admired by the fairy folk that they had granted them special powers. Indeed, Caoilte was one such man and, quite apart from his legendary speed, the fairies had granted him the ability to converse with animals.

One day, Caoilte and his good friend, Cas Corach, set out from their home on the Hill of Allen in search of three hideous werewolves called the Daughters of Airitech. These werewolves lived in a cave close to the ring fort of Ráth Cruachan, the home of the King of Connacht.

On the feast of Samhain every October, the Daughters of Airitech would venture forth from their den in the Cave of Cruachan to gorge on local sheep. In fact, their autumn feasting was causing such great hardship to the local farmers, that the King of Connacht had hired Caoilte to put a stop to it.

The Cave of Cruachan was no ordinary cave. It was an entrance to the otherworld, from which Morrigan, the Goddess of War, was known to occasionally venture forth. No mortal had ever dared to enter the cave, and Caoilte did not intend to be the first. Instead, he planned to draw the sisters out.

The Daughters of Airitech were known to have a weakness for music, and so Caoilte and Cas Corach brought with them a small wire-strung harp. When they reached the Cave of Cruachan, Caoilte called upon all the local birds to fall silent in order that Cas Corach could play a lament.

In the eerie silence of a dawn like no other, the sweet bell-like tones of the harp were carried on the morning mist to the mouth of the cave. Entranced by the beautiful music, the monsters ventured out of the cave, walking one behind the other in single file, as if in a trance.

Seeing them exit the cave, Caoilte cast his spear. It flew through the air with such force that it penetrated the hearts of all three in a single blow, joining them together in death. Their blood gushed forth in a single stream, staining the heather a crimson colour that would endure for seven generations.

Within minutes the ravens of Morrigan arrived in the clouds of a thunderstorm. They came to feast upon the bodies of the dead sisters, and it was as well that they did, for in so doing they prevented them from ever returning in another form.

So ended the tale that Colmán told Gobán on the road to Malahide and, as it did, they found that they had rounded the estuary and reached their destination. Liadin's idea to tell Gobán a story had worked. Neither Colmán nor Gobán had noticed the time passing. The road had been well and truly shortened.

This may well have been the first, but it was not to be the last time that Liadin would come to Colmán's aid. One hundred sunrises later, while Gobán was attempting to teach Colmán his secret method of building a dry-stone wall, she came to his aid again.

Back then people hadn't learnt how to make mortar to stick stones or bricks together. Walls were made by lying stones one upon the other in such a way as they would not easily collapse. This is what we call a dry-stone wall, and it is not as easy as it sounds. Stones come in all shapes and sizes, and it is not easy to lay them in such a manner that the wall will not collapse.

It was Gobán's skill in this art that separated him from all other stonemasons of his day. By his method, walls of enormous height could be built that would never fall down. Alas, one of the keys to laying stones perfectly, was the ability to see a straight line. And Colmán for some reason could not, causing his father's frustration to boil over.

Liadin, witnessing the commotion from her loom, grabbed a ball of wool and tossed it to Gobán. 'Give him the line,' she pleaded. 'For pity sake, Gobán, give him the line.'

Seeing Gobán frozen in a moment of uncertainty, Liadin rose from her knitting, went over to the wall, and stretched a line of wool between two points, to establish a straight line. All Colmán had to do now was to lay the stones in such a way that they did not rise above the line.

Gobán looked on in astonishment. He wondered why *he* had never thought of this, for this method would soon be how bricks were laid all over the world, and it had been invented, not by the great Gobán, but by his daughter-in-law.

Once again, Liadin had proved herself as smart, if not smarter, than Gobán. But then perhaps that was only to be expected, given that she was also the natural daughter of Ráimseach Ruadh. It would not be the last time that Liadin would make a show of her intelligence, but on that day a notion began to take shape in the old man's head – a notion he knew he could never speak of to anyone.

THE SAXON
OUTWITTED

IT HAPPENED ONE day that a wealthy Saxon chieftain from England came to Ireland. His name was Lingle and he had heard such wondrous things about Gobán and the fine buildings and forts he had designed and built, that he wanted him to come to Wiltshire and build a house for him.

But Lingle didn't just want any old house, he wanted a BIG house – a castle, almost. Lingle wanted a building that would be the envy of every King and chieftain in all of England and Ireland. He offered to pay handsomely for such a building – more handsomely than Gobán had ever been paid before – and to supply as many men as it would take to construct it.

Reluctant to turn down the chance of such a lucrative payday, Gobán agreed to take on the job. But, he had one condition. His son, Colmán, must be allowed to come with him, for Colmán had seen little of the world beyond his own shores and the experience would be an education for him. Lingle agreed.

Gobán was excited at the prospect of designing and building so prestigious a building. It would stand as a monument to his skill and ensure that his reputation survived long after his death. His excitement, however, was not shared by his wife.

Ráimseach's heart was filled with foreboding. Despite having met Lingle only the once, she did not trust him. Indeed, she would have pleaded with Gobán to refuse the work, had he not already shaken hands on the deal before she had been introduced to Lingle.

'Promise me,' she said to Colmán on the night before he and his father set off for England, 'that you will use that charming smile of yours to keep in with the Saxon women. Treat them as you would treat your own mother, and talk so freely and honestly with them that they might feel free to talk honestly with you. In that way, you will make friends and will always know what dangers are lying in wait for you. I do not trust this Saxon, Colmán, and it is my dearest desire that you, too, should not trust him, no matter what your father might say.'

'I promise, Mother,' said Colmán. 'I will certainly try my best to do as you ask.'

'I know you will' said his mother with a moist-eyed smile. 'And I shall pray for you both, even though so many of our neighbours have turned to the new god, that I fear the old gods may have already abandoned us to our fate. Nevertheless, on the off-chance that they might still be listening and watching over us, I shall make daily offerings to Manannán, and ask him to bring you safely home to me.'

Lingle's land was situated next to a great forest, and the ready supply of timber meant the work on Lingle's great house progressed much quicker than either he or Gobán had expected. Lingle seemed happy with the progress at first. He even brought some of his friends to watch his new home rise from the ground. But then, just as the roof rafters began to go up, Gobán began to sense a change in him.

'Have you been keeping in with the women?' Gobán asked Colmán one day.

'I have of course,' said Colmán. 'Sure didn't I promise mother that I would?'

'Well then,' said Gobán, 'the time has come to put it to use. Lingle has been behaving very oddly of late. Something sinister is afoot. See what you can find out.'

That day, during the midday lunch break,

Colmán struck up a conversation with the young girl who was serving him his stew.

'Well now,' said Colmán, 'If that isn't the finest stew I've ever tasted. A fine cook like you must be worth a fortune to her master?'

'If only it were true,' said the girl, 'but the master wouldn't know veal from venison. It's all just meat to him. I get paid the same as everyone else in the kitchen, no more and no less.'

'I'm sorry to hear that,' said Colmán. 'But tell me, is there trouble in the household? The master seems out of sorts lately.'

'There is a bit,' said the girl. 'And I shouldn't say any more. Your father has every right to feel proud of his work, everybody says so, but perhaps he has done *too* good a job.'

'*Too* good!' laughed Colmán. 'How could a job of work be considered *too* good?'

'When the master does not want it bettered,' whispered Gretchen in order that the servants would not overhear her. 'The master is so proud of his new house that he does not want to see your father build a better one for someone else. He plans to have your father killed when it is completed. It is the talk of all the household.'

Later that evening, when he was certain they could not be overheard, Colmán told his father what the servant girl had said about Lingle planning to kill them once the building was finished.

'Then it shall never be finished,' said Gobán.

'But if we leave now he'll just come after us,' said Colmán. 'We have no friends in this land. We could never escape.'

'Unless,' said Gobán, 'we give him reason to release us. Today, when we are working on the roof, I shall manufacture a fault that risks the collapse of the whole building.'

'How will that help,' said the son. 'Surely it will only delay the inevitable.'

'Winter is almost here,' said Gobán. 'Lingle will not want us to have to rebuild the roof from

scratch. I shall tell him the tools I need to fix it are back in Ráth Tuirbhí.'

As the day drew to a close and the workmen made their way to the cooking area for their evening meal, Gobán sent a servant to fetch Lingle. When Lingle arrived, Gobán directed his attention to the roof.

'Do you see those cross-beams there,' he said, 'your workmen are not as skilled as my own and they have used a flawed piece of timber at a critical joint. It would take just one icy night for that beam to crack and bring the whole house down. We will have to remove the roof and start again.'

Lingle looked worried. On account of the rapid progress to date, he had made plans to move in before winter. He did not want to have to change them.

'Is there nothing you can do to fix it?' he asked.

'Not immediately,' said Gobán. 'There is a special tool at home in Ireland with which I could

fix it in a couple of hours. But only myself
and my wife know where it is. I will have to go
and fetch it.'

'And leave me with an unfinished house,'
laughed Lingle. 'I don't think so. You and that
boy of yours are not leaving until this house is
finished. I'll send a man to fetch it. Write down
the name of this tool and I'll send him to Ireland
this very day.'

'Do you think my wife is a fool?' said Gobán.
'That tool is a wonder. It took seven years to
make and is worth almost as much as this house
I am building for you. My wife will not hand over
such a rare and valuable thing to a stranger.'

Lingle thought for a moment. The Irishman
had a point. Even if his wife did hand over the
tool to a servant, there was always the danger
that the servant would keep it, or sell it, and not
return to Wiltshire.

'Then I shall send my own son,' said Lingle at
length. 'He will carry a letter from you and you

and your son will remain here under guard until he returns. My men have been given orders to kill you both, should either of you try to escape.'

Gobán had little choice but to accept Lingle's terms. But the name he wrote down, made little sense, even to his own son. In the old Irish script, which Lingle could not read, Gobán had written 'cor in aghaidh a choir, can in aghaidh an chaim'. It meant 'the twist against the turn, and the turn against the twist'.

A tool that twisted in both directions at the same time was obviously impossible, but Lingle did not know that this was what had been written. Gobán was certain, however, that Liadin, at least, would understand his intentions, for he had often seen her observing him work with the same curious intensity with which he had once observed the tradesmen of his own youth. She, he was certain, would know that such a tool was impossible, and the implication that was hidden in the message.

Lingle gave his son, Edgar, enough gold to hire a boat and sent him down to the harbour at Watchet with a servant who was an expert navigator. In the brisk autumn breezes, they fairly flew over the Irish Sea and, just two days later, they rounded Lambay and landed at The Burrow of Portrane.

When Edgar jumped ashore, he was spotted by a member of Gobán's clan who had been out collecting mussels. The local people were accustomed to seeing Saxons, for they often came to trade their pottery and textiles at the emporium on Lambay. But these men were merchants and traders, not finely dressed nobles like Edgar.

Curious as to his identity and his intentions, the mussel collector waited until the Saxons had securely moored their boat before approaching them.

'You there,' he shouted, challenging them at the point of his spear. 'What is your business here?'

'A messenger come from Gobán Saor,' shouted Edgar, signalling to his servant to sheath his sword. 'I seek Ráth Tuirbhí. Can you direct us there?'

'I'm going there myself,' said the mussel collector, re-assured by the re-sheathing of the servant's sword. 'Follow me.'

The mussel collector marched the two Saxons around the estuary and right up to the earthen grassy mounds that enclosed the Ráth Tuirbhí. He then knocked with his spear on the heavy wooden gate that Gobán had built to keep out wolves, and unwanted visitors. Edgar was surprised to find the gate unattended by a gatekeeper. He was even more surprised to find that when the knock was finally answered, it was a servant girl that opened it. Had these people no fear of intruders?

Only when he had entered the compound did Edgar notice the three untethered wolfhounds lapping at their bowls. They growled briefly at him but were quickly silenced by a sharp command from the servant girl as she bolted the gate behind them. The mussel collector, seeing that there were no men about, stood close at hand, just in case he was needed.

Edgar approached the thatched roundhouse that lay at the centre of the compound and knocked on the doorpost, drawing Liadin from her cooking.

'Is this the house of Gobán Saor?' asked Edgar, cautiously looking over her shoulder to a smoky area at the back of the house where someone lay coughing beneath a pile of animal skins.

'It is indeed,' said Liadin. 'And who is it that's asking?'

Only now did Edgar notice that Liadin carried a sheathed knife in her belt. What kind of family was this, he wondered, that even the women carried weapons about their person?

'My name is Edgar, son of Lingle,' said the

young Saxon.

'Well sir,' said Liadin, 'you are welcome here. You speak our language well for a Saxon.'

'I have been to this land many times with my father, but I have come this time at Gobán's bidding. He has sent me to fetch a special tool that he needs to finish my father's house.'

'A tool, you say?' said Liadin, suddenly suspicious. 'Does it have a name, this tool?'

'He had written it down,' said Edgar, handing her a piece of parchment.

'*Cor in aghaidh a choir, can in aghaidh an chaim,*' Liadin read aloud. 'I'm afraid I'm not familiar with this one. Come inside and let me ask my mother-in-law.'

Leaving his servant to wait outside under the watchful eye of the wolfhounds and the mussel collector, Edgar entered the house. As his eyes adjusted to the dark interior he gave a distant, but respectful, bow to the old woman to whom Liadin was bringing the parchment. Women who could read, and women who carried weapons, were not something Edgar was accustomed to. He had heard ancient tales of such women, of course, but had always assumed them to be old wives' tales. He felt suddenly vulnerable.

'I have never heard of such a tool,' whispered Ráimseach to Liadin, 'and this does not make sense. I fear our husbands are in trouble. What should we do?'

'That's exactly what I was thinking myself,' said Liadin. 'But I wanted to be certain that such a tool does not exist because, if it does not, then Gobán is surely telling us that all is not as it should be and that we need to keep the boy here until he can be exchanged for our husbands.'

'But how?' said Ráimseach. 'How are we to capture him? I am much too old and weak to tackle him.'

'Gobán is not a fool,' said Liadin. 'If he has given us the name of a tool, it was surely to direct us to his tool chest. I believe I know what he has in mind, for he has often joked of such a thing.'

Now, against the stone wall of the house there stood the great chest that Gobán had made as a boy and in which he had always kept the most valuable of his many tools. Liadin directed Edgar to it.

'He keeps all of his equipment in that box,' said Liadin. 'The one you want, apparently, has not been used for many years and is probably at the bottom. I am too short to reach that far down. You will have to fetch it yourself.'

'How will I recognise it?' said Edgar.

'It has a gold handle in the form of a serpent,' said Liadin. 'Just be careful you do not break it as you try to retrieve it.'

As Edgar leaned over the edge of the chest, stretching to reach the bottom, Liadin grabbed hold of his free foot and tipped him in. Quick as a whip, she slammed the lid closed and sat on it. Ráimseach, rising from her bed, ran to help her lock the chest.

Having caught his breath, Edgar called out for his servant, who immediately came running, followed after by the mussel collector. Grabbing a spear from the weapons rack, Liadin moved to meet him. The servant stopped dead in his tracks as he recognised that he was trapped, one spear before him and another behind.

'You have been outwitted young man,' said Liadin, 'and if you do not wish to die here this day, you will leave immediately and tell Lingle that, until our husbands return with the gold they were promised for their work, his son will never leave this chest alive. Make haste now. You might still beat the turn of the tide.'

When the servant returned empty-handed, Lingle realised that he had been beaten and had little option but to release Gobán and his son. Gobán, for his part, gave Lingle his word that he would see to it that Edgar was returned unharmed.

Gobán and Colmán returned to Ráth Tuirbhí a

few days later, and Lingle's son was released. The Saxon's house, in consequence, was never finished. The following year, however, the Saxons invaded the Kingdom of Brega from their base on the Isle of Man. They burned several churches and took many hostages.

No reason was ever given for the attack, but no one who lived anywhere near to Ráth Tuirbhí had any doubt that it was in revenge for the humiliation inflicted upon the Saxons by Gobán and his family, who survived the invasion by hiding in the darkest parts of the wildest woods, where few others would dare to go.

They remained in the woods, and hidden from the outside world, until the Saxon war drums and battle horns fell silent, at which time they returned to Ráth Tuirbhí. Their return, however, was not universally welcomed, and they found themselves no longer well-regarded by their Christian neighbours, many of whom had lost friends and family to the Saxons.

Indeed many of their neighbours, to whom they had once felt so close, now began to look upon them as selfish pagans; as an elitist family who had always been more concerned with proving their own cleverness than with the consequences of their actions. Ráth Tuirbhí soon became a lonely place, seldom visited and cursed with bitterness and regret.

GOBÁN THE BLIND

THE WORLD WAS changing. Respect for the old ways was slowly dying. Clients no longer treated Gobán as a highly skilled artisan, but as a common tradesman. This was especially true at the monasteries, where the monks regarded him as an inferior on account of his pagan beliefs.

This lack of respect so angered Gobán that he began to charge the monks far more than he charged anyone else for his services. If he could no longer have their esteem, he reasoned angrily, then he would at least have a share of their great wealth.

Indeed, were it not for Ráimseach, his wife, whose soothing words kept him from consistently falling out with clients, he would have had no work at all. Old age was not being kind to the great Gobán Saor.

When Ráimseach died, Gobán began almost impossible to work with. Taking his grief and anger out on the world, he would annoy his clients by demanding outrageous prices for his services, sometimes even raising the price after the work had started.

His behaviour won him few friends, and many enemies. But there was still no better builder in all the land and, if you wanted a great monastery built, and built to last, then Gobán Saor was your only man.

One day an abbot in the south of the country engaged Gobán to rebuild a bell tower that had been destroyed by raiders from a rival monastery. Gobán decided not only to rebuild the tower, but to redesign it. Indeed he set about building the new tower so high that, even before it was finished, the like of it was not to be found anywhere in these islands.

But then, one day, while Gobán was resting inside the tower, he happened to overhear himself being spoken of in a very disrespectful manner by several of the monks who were sitting outside and unaware of his presence.

Angered by what he overheard, Gobán stormed out of the tower. His cheeks flushed with rage, he went straight to the abbot and raised the price. Instead of four cows, he now insisted, he wanted eight.

But the abbot, an old greybeard who was almost as stubborn as Gobán himself, refused to pay. They had shaken hands on an agreement. He was not going to renegotiate it now on account of Gobán's injured pride.

In a raging temper, Gobán marched out of the abbot's room and went straight to the top of the bell tower to retrieve his tools. Certain that

Gobán was preparing to leave, and that the tower would be left unfinished, the abbot waited until he had reached the top, then took away the ladder.

'We shook hands on a price,' the abbot shouted up to him. 'So you will take what we agreed, or you can remain where you are until the ravens pick you clean. You will soon see, Gobán Saor, that I am not a man to be trifled with.'

But Gobán was not to be pacified. 'You will pay what I'm worth,' he shouted angrily back, 'and you, too, will find that, as old as I am, that I am not a man to be trifled with. You will find that I can shout as loud as any bell and that neither you nor your congregation will ever pray undisturbed as long as I am up here.'

With neither side willing to budge, Gobán remained stuck in the tower for two days with only the rainwater to sustain him. On the third day, just as the sun was rising, an old beggar passed by on the road below. Gobán shouted after him.

'Old man!' bellowed Gobán. 'Where might you be travelling to?'

'Wherever the road takes me,' said the beggar.

'Could I perhaps persuade you to take a message to my son?' said Gobán. 'You will be well rewarded for your trouble. My name is Gobán Saor, and I'm being kept here against my will.'

'And against your famous wits, it seems' said the beggar. 'Why don't you just come down?'

'They've taken the ladder away,' said Gobán, 'and I am far too old to survive a jump.'

'So the great Gobán Saor is finally trapped,' the beggar laughed. 'I never thought I'd live to see the day.'

'Well old I may be,' laughed Gobán, 'but I am not so proud as to be incapable of asking for help.'

'Then consider this,' said the old beggar. 'If *you* cannot come down, then surely the *tower* must, for it is surely as easy to throw down two stones as to carry up one. Indeed, I would imagine it is

much, much faster."

Gobán reached into his purse and tossed down two pieces of silver to the old man.

'Thank you,' he said, 'Anger had made me blind. But I can see clearly now.'

Over the course of the following hour, Gobán began to dismantle the tower, taking one stone at a time and dropping it to the ground so that a pile began to form at the base. Had he been allowed to continue, the tower would have continued to shrink until it reached the rising pile of stones, at which point he would have been able to scramble down.

But Gobán had only succeeded in lowering the tower by a few feet before the monks, alerted by the sound of crashing stones, came running. Recognising that he had been outsmarted, and to prevent Gobán from totally demolishing the tower, the abbot ordered the ladder to be brought back.

When Gobán came down, the abbot promised

to pay him what he'd asked for, as long as the tower was completed. Gobán, however, had had enough. His eyes burning with anger, he left without being paid and without finishing the tower, which served only to annoy the monks even more.

'That pagan needs teaching a lesson,' one of them growled. The others agreed.

A group of monks quickly formed and set out after Gobán. He had insulted their abbot, and he had insulted their church. He was too influential a person to be allowed to behave like that. He had to be punished, at the very least to deter others from following his example.

And so, late that evening, as day deepened into night and Gobán was making his way home along a forest track, he found himself set upon by the monks and his eyes put out. Totally blind, he was forced to crawl along the forest floor, feeling his way forward, calling out for assistance but never entirely sure of where he was going. At length the blood loss caused him to lose consciousness.

When finally he woke, Gobán could not tell if it was night or day, for all was darkness to him now. He guessed it must be morning by the feel of the cold dank air on his clothes and the weak heat of what he assumed to be the rising sun on his skin.

He struggled to his feet and attempted to feel his way out of the forest, but he stumbled so often on the tangled roots of the trees that he once again had to resort to crawling on all fours like a helpless infant.

The forest was unusually quiet. It was almost as if the whole of nature was still in a state of shock from having witnessed an act of such horrific violence and barbarity. Every now and then there would be a rustle of leaves and the flap of a startled woodpigeon. It was a sound that Gobán knew only too well, a sound that could so easily alert a lurking wolf to his presence.

For the first time in his life, Gobán felt vulnerable in a forest. Quite apart from the animals he disturbed with his movement, his face and clothes were still sticky with drying blood, the scent of which he knew could also attract a hungry wolf.

But then, all of a sudden, carried erratically on the gentle breeze that snatched at his wispy grey beard, there came the sound of a young girl singing. He could not determine how far distant she was, but he could determine the direction. And so he attempted to crawl towards her and to call out for assistance, but the wind was in his face and his weak voice refused to carry.

It was quite a while before she heard him and stopped singing, only to resume again. He called out again, and again, until the little strength he had left began to wane. He might well have died, had the girl's curiosity not finally gotten the better of her and, despite the repeated warnings of her parents, went to investigate. Finding him, she screamed, and the scream brought her parents running to her side.

For the many days that Gobán remained as a guest in the woodman's hut, he never let on who he was, or how he had come about his wounds. The family fed him, washed his clothes, bathed his wounds, and bandaged the sockets of his eyes. But even though they were poor, they never once tried to take advantage of him or steal from his purse.

His waking hours were a torture to him, for every helpless moment of them was a reminder of what he had lost. From being the greatest builder that Ireland had ever known, he would be reduced now to a simple craftsman, carving by touch, a maker of spoons and axe shafts. He was not certain he could endure the humiliation.

Only in sleep did Gobán find any comfort, for in his dreams he could still see the haunts of his childhood – the hazel woods of Turvey and, increasingly, the sandy Burrow of Portrane, where the selkies would occasionally come ashore to take human form for a night. With each successive dream, his longing for home grew steadily stronger. It was almost as if the selkies themselves were calling him.

When Gobán had recovered enough to travel, a young boy and a horse were hired to guide him home. Before mounting the saddle, he paused to reward the family who had cared for him with several pieces of gold ring money. It was then, and only then, that they learnt his name.

Once Gobán was back on the road, he was quickly recognised and word of both his presence and the state of his health travelled quickly before him. News eventually reached a kind abbot who took pity on Gobán and offered him shelter. His name was Abbán, and one night over dinner he asked Gobán to build him a monastery.

'But I have no eyes!' laughed Gobán. 'It is impossible to do as you ask. Utterly impossible.'

The abbot rose from his seat and approached Gobán. Laying his hand over Gobán's empty eye sockets he declared – 'Let the Lord grant thee sight whilst thou art about the work of the Lord, and take it back when thy work is done.'

When Abbán removed his hand, Gobán found that he could see. His eyes were still missing, but he could see. It made no sense but, hoping all the while that the condition might yet prove permanent, he stayed many moons with Abbán and helped him to build his new monastery.

But then, just as Abbán had predicted, the morning after the monastery was completed Gobán woke up blind. A horse and guide were again hired, and Gobán left Wexford that same day, filled with a renewed urge to make his way home to Ráth Tuirbhí.

Somewhere along the road, alas, Gobán's empty eye sockets fell prey to an infection. It took so grave a hold of him that his guide felt compelled to lead him to the monastery at

Derrynaflan, County Tipperary, where, on seeing his condition, the monks sent a messenger to Ráth Tuirbhí to advise his family to come at once.

When Colmán and his wife, Liadin, arrived at Derrynaflan, they found the white-haired old builder lying on a straw mattress looking sickly and thin but clinging desperately to life. Lacking the strength to raise himself from his pillow, he had to be lifted into a sitting position to greet them.

The room was dark, lit only by the light of a fire that was burning in the next room. Gobán did not even have a candle, the monks being reluctant to waste one on a blind man. A sharp word from Liadin, however, was enough to send one scurrying to fetch one. Noting the sharpness of her tone, Gobán made as if to say something, but it came to nothing.

Liadin could see that Gobán was dying, and quickly realised that his trade secrets were about to be lost forever. She encouraged him to try one last time to explain them to Colmán, but the old man had long since given up on trying to teach his son.

Then Liadin had an idea. If appealing to the old man's love for his son was not enough to prise his secrets from him, she would try appealing to his vanity. And so, the following morning, as she brought him his milk, she also brought an allegation so outrageous that Gobán would feel compelled to defend himself.

'The abbey at Mag Arnaide has fallen,' she said without even a hint of insincerity. 'It came down last night in high winds.'

'Impossible,' said Gobán, taking the bait, 'for I built those walls myself, putting a stone in, a stone out, and a stone across, putting one stone upon two, and two stones upon three. Those walls could never have fallen. Someone must have weakened them.'

'A jealous builder, perhaps,' said Liadin,

'trying to work out your secret.'

'Or a secret daughter,' said Gobán with a weak smile, 'trying to protect her husband.'

'Ah!' sighed Liadin. 'So 'tis true. I have long suspected as much. How long have you known?'

'From the day you first stepped foot in my house,' said Gobán, 'I have suspected you were hers. You could have been sisters you were so alike. But it was not until your cleverness began to show itself that I began to suspect you could also be mine. Come closer child. We have much to discuss.'

Over the course of the several hours, Gobán taught Liadin all of his secrets and, when he was done, he lay back on his pillow, exhausted. His voice quickly became weak and his breathing shallow. The hand of death had been laid upon his shoulder. He knew his time was short.

'I have one last request to make of you,' he said to Liadin. 'The secret of your birth, and that of your husband, is now yours to keep. Promise me that you will keep it as long as your husband lives. He must never know.'

'I love him,' said Liadin. 'I would never hurt him so. The secret, I assure you, is safe with me.'

'Then all is settled,' sighed Gobán. 'You can send for him now.'

And with that Gobán fell into a deep sleep from which he would never waken. He died peacefully, knowing that his secrets were safely stored in the head of his talented daughter.

Gobán was buried, not at Ráth Tuirbhí, but at Derrynaflan, the former being too far distant to carry a dead body. Not being a Christian, he could not be buried within the church grounds, and so they buried him on a piece of land just outside the cemetery. His grave is still there and remembered to this day.

Liadin and Colmán returned to Ráth Tuirbhí, but Liadin never managed to make a skilled tradesman of her husband and had instead to educate his workers in Gobán's methods and the

Bearla Lagair. Had she not done so, the family would not have been able to continue in the building trade.

But each man she trained passed the secrets to his sons, and each son to his sons, until Gobán's methods, and his secret language, became the secret of stonemasons throughout the entire country, and beyond.

Appendix

THE REAL GOBÁN

'Traigh Tuirbe. How did it get its name? It is not difficult to say. Tuirbe Tragmár, father of Gobán, it was he that owned the strand, and the land.

It was he that used to throw a cast of his axe from Tuladh-an-Bhiail into the face of the flowing tide, and it would stop the sea from flowing, and the sea would not come past it.

His true pedigree is not known, unless he was one of the disgraced men of art who fled out of Tara before the Samildánach, and who remain in the wastelands of Brega.'

The Edinburgh Dinnshenchas.

IN ANCIENT IRELAND, the Kingdom of Turvey, or *Tuath Tuirbhe*, was a minor coastal kingdom north of Dublin with its own chieftain or lord. The shores of this kingdom, known then as *Traigh Tuirbhe*, stretched from the Rogerstown Estuary in the north to the Broadmeadow Estuary in the south, and possibly beyond.

The modern townland of Turvey, in Donabate, derives its name from this kingdom, a place that was famously celebrated in an eight-century poem by the poet Mac Samáin, as being a heavily wooded area of hazel trees and blackberry bushes:

Let none hold dear the wood of Fuirmhe,
Where it grows about Tuirbhe;
Its leaves wound me,
Its thicket does not shelter me.

In the ancient *Annals of the Four Masters*, we are told that the 'youths of Turvey' were once involved in the slaying of King Colmán Rímid in the year 604. The same annals also mention the death of 'Ainniarraidh, the son of Maelmuire, Lord of Turvey' as having taken place in the year 898.

Tuath Tuirbhe, therefore, would appear to have existed for at least three hundred years, and possibly much longer than that. All that remains today, however, is a townland near the village of Donabate.

In 1899, workmen digging the foundations for St. Ita's Hospital in Portrane uncovered an underground tomb with a long approach tunnel that was lined with stones. Inside the main chamber, they came upon the skeleton of a large man that many at the time believed to have been the remains of real Tuirbe Trágmar or 'Turvey of the Strands'.

Unfortunately, such was the poor regard for ancient monuments back then, that the entire structure was reputedly cleared away by workmen and the skeleton thrown on a bank of rubbish. It is not known if the remains were ever re-buried.

The tale of Tuirbe and his enchanted axe may well have been nothing more than a myth, but his alleged son, Gobán, was very real indeed. Regarded in folklore as the greatest Irish architect of the seventh century, the life of Gobán Saor became heavily mythologised following his death, which occurred sometime in the late seventh century.

Born in Turvey, in north County Dublin, sometime about the year 560, Gobán was employed by many Irish saints to build their churches and oratories. What few records remain of his existence appear to suggest that he was an architectural genius well ahead of his time.

The real Gobán is first mentioned in an eight-century Irish poem attributed to a lunatic protected by St. Moling, which is preserved at the monastery of St. Paul in Lavanttal, Austria. Written just a century after his death, the poem mentions Gobán as the builder of a fort at Túaim Inbir in Co. Westmeath.

The real Gobán is also mentioned in the *Life of St. Aidan of Ferns* (who died in 632 CE) as having been employed by Saint Aidan to build a stone church. The saint's successor, Mochua of Luachair is also recorded as having employed him, this time to build a wooden church.

The biography that contains the most information about the real Gobán, however, is that of Saint Moling, who died in the year 690. After the fall of the Eó Rossa, the famous yew tree celebrated in the *Book of Leinster*, some of the wood is recorded in Moling's biography as having been given by him to Gobán to build an oratory with.

Apart from the many stories that have been told about him, Gobán's name has also been immortalised in many Irish placenames. In the parish of Ramoan in County Antrim, for example, there is a building called 'Gobbin's Heir's Castle'. The parish of Kilgobbin, in Rathdown, Co. Dublin, is also believed to have taken its name from him.

According to tradition, Gobán was buried at Derrynaflan, in County Tipperary. His wife, who died before him, was buried elsewhere. In a section of the Annals of Ulster, recording the plundering of Dowth by the Danes, one of the plundered sites is described as 'the grave of the wife of Gobán'.

After his death, many of the stories told about Gobán spread throughout the country and were heavily localised in the telling. In this book, I have reversed the trend and reclaimed them for the people of the peninsula on which Gobán was born. I have also rewritten them in the style of a biography and given names to many of the characters who had been left nameless in the old tales.

I hope you have enjoyed reading about Gobán, and that, when next you visit the beautiful Portrane Peninsula, you will remember the most famous man to have been born there and will see in its jagged shoreline, not just a string of unconnected beaches, but the continuous *Traigh Tuirbe* of legend.

In the *Life of St. Abbán*, it was prophesied that the fame of Gobán, as a builder in wood and stone, would exist in Ireland to the end of time. I hope this book helps in some small way to do that. These stories are, after all, a part of our shared heritage and, indeed, our history.

ACKNOWLEDGMENTS

I am firstly indebted to my schoolteachers at Marymount Primary School in Harold's Cross, Dublin, who, during the 1960s, enthusiastically imparted so many Irish legends to children like myself, including several tales of Gobán Saor. Their names and faces have long since faded from memory, but the stories they told live on.

I am also indebted to Zoe Stephenson for her editorial assistance and advice, and similarly to Anne Bermingham and her 6th class students at Scoil Phádraic Cailíní in Donabate, for having test-read an early draft of the book. Many thanks are also due to Derry Dillon for his wonderful illustrations and Marcel Koortzen for proofreading the finished work.

Especial gratitude is also due to Helen O'Donnell, Betty Boardman, and the staff of the County Archives in Fingal County Council, for their continued support, over several years now, of my efforts to document the lives and legends of the Portrane Peninsula. Finally, I owe the usual debt of gratitude to my wife, Cliona, and daughter, Eleanor, for their continued forbearance and support.

TALES OF OLD TURVEY

OTHER BOOKS
IN THE SAME SERIES

The Legend of Joseph Daw

GERARD RONAN

Illustrated by Derry Dillon

Rescued from a shipwreck at the age of four, Joseph Daw is taken as an unpaid servant by a family of smugglers from Turvey, a townland in north County Dublin close to the village of Donabate. Despite a life of hardship and cruelty, he grows up to be a quiet and honest youth, very different from his masters. But, just as he finds the courage to escape, he chances to witness an event that changes everything, and not for the better.

The Old Man and the Tower

GERARD RONAN

Illustrated by Derry Dillon

Twelve-year-old Rufus has been disqualified from a National Short Story competition. The judges have accused him of copying the story of a child who won the competition twelve years earlier. But Rufus's story was not a work of fiction. It was a true account of his encounters with a mysterious old man who spoke in riddles – a man who had taken to hanging about the Martello Tower in Donabate the previous summer.

But how could that be? How could two children have shared an identical experience twelve years apart? And why did they both choose to write about it? And why, when the two eventually meet, will the encounter change both of their lives forever?

Lucky Kate

GERARD RONAN

Illustrated by Derry Dillon

Orphaned and homeless at the age of sixteen, Kate Ryan is sent to the county workhouse at Balrothery where, after three years of picking oakum, she is offered the opportunity of a lifetime.

To save on the cost of caring for them, the workhouse guardians are offering to pay the passage of three young women to the new colonies in Australia, where there is a shortage of women. Tickets have already been booked for them on the largest passenger ship ever built – the *Tayleur*. It is a voyage that will change Kate's life forever.

Printed in Great Britain
by Amazon